THE END OF THE SADDLE CLUB?

Lisa and Stevie each knew what the other was thinking. They ought to have gone to Pine Hollow. Stevie spoke first. "Uh, I better hang up. My mom will be home soon, and I'll be in big trouble if she thinks I watched TV all day."

"I have to go, too," Lisa said. "But, hey," she added, remembering her new role as Stevie's coach, "I'll see you tomorrow, bright and early!"

After putting the phone down, Lisa stared up at her picture of The Saddle Club and their horses. Horse-crazy? she thought. They sure weren't acting it. Willing to help each other out in any situation? While Carole was helping out, the two of them were sitting at home. "But we always help out!" Lisa wailed. "Why can't someone else help out for a while?" The picture didn't answer. It just stared back at her accusingly. How long would she and Stevie go, it seemed to ask, breaking both rules of The Saddle Club?

THE SADDLE CLUB

HORSE FEVER

BONNIE BRYANT

A SKYLARK BOOK
NEW YORK • TORONTO • LONDON • SYDNEY • AUCKLAND

RL 5, 009–012

HORSE FEVER

A Bantam Skylark Book / January 1999

ISBN 0-553-48635-7

Published simultaneously in the United States and Canada.

PRINTED IN THE UNITED STATES OF AMERICA

OPM   0 9 8 7 6 5 4 3 2 1

I would like to express my special thanks
to Caitlin Macy for her
help in the writing of this book.

DIMLY, FROM FAR away, Stevie Lake heard a noise. A loud noise. A loud, insistent, blaring noise that might have been an alarm clock. Her alarm clock. It *might* have been. She couldn't be sure, of course. It was probably better to ignore it. *Who knows? Maybe it'll go away.* She rolled over in bed and clamped a pillow to her head. Unfortunately the blare seemed to get louder. Then another noise was added to it. It was the sound of yelling: boys' yelling.

"Stevie! Stevie, wake up!"

"Stevie, we're late!"

"Stevie, get up! You overslept!"

A hand on her arm jarred Stevie out of her half sleep. Blinking and rubbing her eyes, she struggled to sit up.

1

What she saw was not her idea of a pleasant awakening: Her three brothers, Chad, Michael, and Alex, were standing beside her bed. "Stevie!" Alex cried, his voice desperate. "We've gotta hurry! We all overslept and we're late for school!"

"You mean we—"

"The car pool left without us!" Chad interrupted.

"Mom says we've gotta walk!" Michael cried.

Instantly Stevie's mood changed from mild annoyance to utter panic. She had been late to school three times already—one more and she'd have to stay after. She sprang from her bed. "I'll meet you downstairs in two minutes!" she yelled, shooing the boys out.

"All right, but hurry!" Alex urged again.

Thank God for brothers, Stevie thought, running to the closet. Now that she was awake she dimly remembered hitting the Snooze button—ten or eleven times.

Stevie threw open her closet doors. A gargantuan pile of dirty clothes spilled out—jeans, turtlenecks, socks, underwear, skirts, and blouses. She riffled through the mostly empty hangers in desperation. "My kingdom for some clean clothes!" she cried, charging out into the hall. If by some miracle she could find something in the dryer, she swore she would never, ever play a trick on her brothers again, never turn up her nose at broccoli—

"Watch where you're going, Steph—!"

2

"Aaahhh!"

In her haste to get to the laundry room, Stevie ran smack-dab into her mother. Mrs. Lake put a settling hand on her daughter's shoulder. "What's your hurry, dear?"

"Oh, Mom, I'm in major trouble!" Stevie began. "I'm late for school and I can't find anything to wear and—" In the middle of her breathless explanation, Stevie noticed something. Her mother was wearing a bathrobe. Stevie hardly ever saw her mother in a bathrobe. Mrs. Lake was always up and dressed before the rest of the family. She left for work when her children left for school. The only time she hung out in her bathrobe was on . . .

"*Saturday!*" Stevie screamed, a horrible realization dawning on her.

"Yes, dear, I know it's Saturday," Mrs. Lake began, "and we're going to make cookies—" But Stevie was already halfway down the stairs.

"You're dead meat!" she shrieked.

Chad, Michael, and Alex ran for cover in the basement. "Barricade the door!" Chad yelled.

Stevie stopped short as the door closed in her face. "You're just lucky I didn't start on the way to school!" she growled. "You're dead as it is, but if I had walked to Fenton, you'd be even deader!"

On the other side of the door, Stevie's brothers howled with laughter. "As if you could walk to school!" came

Alex's muffled voice. "It would take you so long the day would be over!"

Stevie's eyes narrowed. There were some offenses that could not go unpunished. As she looked around for a suitable chair to use as a battering ram, her father appeared in the hallway. "*Pssst!* Come on!" he urged. "I got a dozen doughnuts and you can have first dibs!"

Stevie hesitated, watching her father disappear into the kitchen. She was trapped, caught between her desire to murder her twin, Alex, on the spot, and her desire to eat all the honey-dipped doughnuts and leave only the jelly ones for her brothers. Chad and Michael were as obnoxious as ever, but *Alex* . . . Lately Alex was even more insufferable. Ever since he had taken up track and basketball at Fenton, he was constantly going on about what great shape he was in. "You call that a sport!" he would say about horseback riding, Stevie's athletic activity. *It isn't fair*, Stevie thought grumpily. *Riding gets no respect, fitness-wise. Everyone thinks you just sit there* . . .

"Riding!" Stevie clapped a hand to her mouth, remembering. That was why her alarm had been set in the first place. She had a lesson that morning—a dressage lesson and the first lesson since Christmas. Warning of future vengeance on her siblings, she ran back up the stairs. Halfway up, though, she felt her energy sag. In her bedroom she sat down on the bed, fighting off the temptation to curl up under the covers. For some reason, she felt more like eating doughnuts, going back to sleep, making cookies with her mom—any and all of the above—than having a riding lesson. She dragged herself up and went over to the massive laundry pile. It was no surprise that each pair of jeans was filthier than the last, and that her sole pair of breeches was even worse. Riding all the time generated a *lot* of dirty clothes, and Mrs. Lake was adamant about her children doing their own laundry. With a sigh Stevie picked up the least offensive pair and went to the bathroom to sponge off the stains. *Maybe*, she thought grimly, *this is what they mean by waking up on the wrong side of the bed.* It sure felt like it, anyway. She was tired before the day had even started!

LISA ATWOOD HAD her nose in a book. She could hear her mother honking in the driveway, but she ignored it. If she could just get to the end of chapter three . . . The horn sounded again, more insistent this time. With a loud, long-suffering sigh, Lisa slapped shut *To Kill a Mockingbird*. She grabbed her gloves off the side table and ran for the car. "Coming, Mom!"

Riding over to Pine Hollow, Lisa gave in to her bad mood. Here it was, Christmas vacation, and she had more homework than ever. Lately the teachers seemed to view vacation as an excuse to heap on more work. It made it so that even homework she normally would have enjoyed, like reading *To Kill a Mockingbird*, became a chore.

And naturally, just when Lisa was feeling swamped at school, her mother started piling on the tasks at home. ". . . and you need to get a haircut," Mrs. Atwood was saying. "You also need to exchange the dress Aunt Meg and Uncle Bob gave you. And have you written your thank-you notes yet?"

"No," Lisa muttered grumpily. Only *her* mother would ask a question like that so soon after the holiday!

"But you'll start them today?" Mrs. Atwood prompted.

"Yes, Mom," Lisa said wearily.

"Good," said her mother, looking pleased. "Don't forget Mrs. Chambers. She gave you the needlepoint kit."

Lisa let out a loud sigh. The winter before, she had learned embroidery to please her mother. This year her mother's friend Mrs. Chambers had given her a needlepoint kit. Would the arts and crafts never end?

"What's wrong, dear? I thought you liked needlepoint. And this pattern is so cute, right up your alley with the horse heads and the blue ribbons. Celeste was so nice to pick it out specially for you."

Lisa did have to admit she liked the pattern. And she was pretty good at needlepoint. But right now it just felt like another chore.

"You could finish it and give it to one of your friends for her birthday," Mrs. Atwood persisted.

"That's a good idea," Lisa said to satisfy her mother. It would certainly be an unusual gift. Stevie or Carole would never be caught dead doing needlepoint!

"Now what about the haircut? When should I make your appointment? I hope Charles can fit you in before school starts. Of course," Mrs. Atwood added pointedly, "it would be easier if you didn't spend every waking moment at Pine Hollow . . ."

Lisa was too tired to argue with her mother's favorite complaint. The truth was, Lisa knew how much easier her life would have been if she hadn't been totally horse-crazy. She would have had more time for homework, more time for school activities, more time to relax, even. And relaxing, as Lisa had learned the hard way, was an important "activity" for an overachiever like herself.

"I'll tell you what," Mrs. Atwood remarked. "*I* have an appointment today. It's my weekly wash and style. Why don't you take it, dear? I can skip a week; my hair ought to hold out all right. I could pick you up right after your lesson, on my way back from the supermarket. How does that sound?" Lisa's mother looked expectantly at her.

Lisa opened her mouth to protest, but then she stopped. Normally she and her two best friends, Stevie

Lake and Carole Hanson, hung out at Pine Hollow after their lessons. They would clean tack, fuss over their horses, and help out with whatever work needed to be done around the barn. Today, the first Saturday after Christmas, there would be lots of work. Their instructor and the owner of the stables, Max Regnery, probably had a list of chores a mile long. Or if he didn't, his mother, Mrs. Reg, would. Mrs. Reg could always find things for the girls to do. For some reason the thought annoyed Lisa that morning. *Maybe,* she thought defensively, *I just don't feel like cleaning tack today.* For a moment she allowed herself to visualize her other option: sitting in a salon chair having her hair washed. Soaking in the ambience at Cosmo Cuts. Flipping through the teen magazines her mother never let her buy. The picture brought a smile to her lips. She could get the special conditioning treatment, the cut and style, the blow-dry . . .

Lisa never skimped, not on anything, especially not on anything to do with horses. If she had, she wouldn't have been a member of The Saddle Club, the group she, Stevie, and Carole had started. Still, her friends would understand if she had to leave early just this once. "All right, Mom," she said before she had time to feel guilty, "that sounds good."

* * *

CAROLE HANSON WAS the first member of The Saddle Club to arrive at Pine Hollow. She almost always was. Even though all three girls were horse-crazy—being horse-crazy and being willing to help one another out were the two requirements of the club—Carole was a bit crazier. She was passionate about horses. Per her request, her father had dropped her off a full hour before the lesson was to begin.

After giving her horse, Starlight, a good grooming, Carole headed to the tack room to get the gelding's saddle and bridle, whistling on the way. She had an entire day to spend at the barn, and she couldn't wait to saddle up. She was going to give Starlight a nice long warm-up to get the kinks out before their dressage lesson. Starlight had been given a few days off over Christmas, and Carole knew he would have some extra energy. If she didn't work it off before the lesson, he would be skittish in front of Max. Carole always knew when the gelding was going to act up. She knew his faults to a tee—which wasn't surprising, since she had trained him. It was part of what made them such great partners.

The tack room was empty and quiet. Carole was about to load up with tack when something caught her eye. It was the new edition of *Horseman's Weekly*. She sat down on a tack trunk to take a quick peek. She liked to thumb through the paper. First she would skim the horse show results to see if she recognized any names. Then she would read "Pony Club News." Finally she would take the horseman's quiz at the back.

This week's issue was pretty slim, though. It was January, so there weren't many competitions to cover. Ditto "Pony Club News." And the quiz was too easy. As if, Carole thought indignantly, there was anyone out there who didn't know that the walk had four beats; the trot, two; and the canter, three. *Please!* Idly Carole scanned the "Hunt Club News" and the advertisements. She didn't usually bother with the ads. She wasn't looking for a horse, after all. But they could be interesting to read. It was fun to imagine what kind of person would be looking for what kind of horse.

" 'Ten-point-two Shetland,' " Carole read aloud, " 'goes English and Western, drives, Pony Clubs.' " That was an easy call. A pony like that would go to a little boy or girl looking for a first horse—bought by a parent who put safety first. The ad below the Shetland was completely different: " 'Superbly talented four-year-old jumper,' " Carole read. That was a horse that would probably go to a professional—somebody like Max, Carole mused, a rider who wanted a horse that could be trained to win, then resold at a profit.

Curious now, Carole read on. There was an Arabian

that sounded like a nice trail horse; an Appaloosa that had won at barrel racing; a seasoned hunter; an unbroken yearling colt. There really seemed to be a horse for every kind of rider under the sun. That was what made horses so fascinating, Carole thought. You could never get to know all of them. The types were endless.

"Carole, you here yet?"

Stevie's voice startled Carole out of her reverie. "I'm in the tack room!" she called.

A moment later Stevie burst in. "Belle's a mess," she announced. "She looks like she's been rolling in mud for three straight days." Belle was Stevie's horse, a Saddlebred-Arabian cross.

"I hate to say it," Carole joked, "but she probably has been."

"I know, I know—the pastures are muddy swamps from all the rain," Stevie said, flopping down beside Carole. She peered over Carole's shoulder. "What's this? Oh, cool! The new *Horseman's Weekly*. Are you looking for a new horse?"

"Of course not!" Carole retorted. "I was just looking at the ads for fun!"

Stevie gave her friend a strange look. "I was just kidding, Carole," she said.

11

"OH—RIGHT," SAID Carole, embarrassed.

"Maybe I should trade Belle in," Stevie joked, "and get a horse that doesn't like mud!"

Now Carole laughed for real. Everyone knew that such a horse didn't exist. "Let's see . . . who would you buy?" she asked. "The 'superbly talented four-year-old?' "

"Nah—too green." Stevie leaned over the newspaper, reading. "Hmmm . . . How about this one: 'sixteen-point-two hand, eight-year-old Dutch warmblood. Experienced, high-level dressage horse. Big, floating trot—' "

Carole leaned in, too. "Wait, where's that one? I didn't see it before."

Stevie pointed to the ad. "Sounds pretty nice, huh?"

"Yeah," said Carole, surprised that she had missed it.

"Especially for today's dressage lesson," Stevie added. "I love dressage, but I'm sick of it! The Saddlebred in Belle may love the ring, but the Arabian in her wants to be out on the trail. And lately the Arabian is winning!"

"Now, Stevie," said Carole, assuming a teacherly tone, "flatwork is good for you. Walking, trotting, cantering, figure eights, bending, lengthening and shortening the stride—those are the fundamentals of all equitation. Until one masters—"

"Yeah, yeah," Stevie interrupted, a touch crossly. "I know dressage is good for you. But today I'd just rather . . . go on a trail ride, okay?" With that she rose, picked up her saddle, and slung Belle's bridle over her shoulder. Sometimes Carole's enthusiasm for everything to do with horses got the tiniest bit annoying. Carole would never have understood about wanting to stay home and sleep in. She would never have wanted to make cookies instead of going to the barn. She just didn't think like that. Starlight was her whole life.

"Do you want to come tack up with me?" Stevie asked, softening her tone.

"In a sec," Carole replied. "I—uh—I'll be there in a sec."

After Stevie had gone, Carole picked up *Horseman's*

Weekly again. She started to skim the ad columns for the warmblood's ad.

"Hi, Carole!" called a voice. This time it was Lisa, stopping by to get Prancer's tack. Hastily Carole closed the newspaper as Lisa stepped through the door.

"Are you going to enter the contest?" Lisa inquired.

"What contest?" said Carole, confused.

"Oh, well, I see you're reading *Horseman's Weekly*. They're sponsoring their annual writing contest. Here, let me see."

Carole handed the newspaper to Lisa, who thumbed the pages till she found the ad she was looking for. "See? " 'Annual short story contest . . . This year's topic: Write a story or the first chapter of a novel about a horse and rider facing a turning point . . . word limit: fifteen hundred . . .' Well, you can read it for yourself."

"Are you entering?" asked Carole. It sounded perfect for Lisa.

"I don't know. I'm so busy. . . . I can't really think of anything to write about, either. But you should enter, Carole."

"You think so?"

Lisa shrugged. "Why not? It won't take that much work, and the prize is usually a new saddle." She folded the newspaper in half and laid it on a trunk. "Ready?"

"Ah . . . yeah," said Carole, eyeing the paper.

14

"Oh, I'm sorry. Is that yours? I thought it was the Pine Hollow copy."

"It is," said Carole, embarrassed again. "It is. I was just . . . reading it."

DRESSAGE. SOME PEOPLE pronounced it dress*age*. Some people said *dress*age. Either way, the goal was the same: to get the horse and rider moving in harmony. The horse was supposed to be supple, balanced, and attentive to its rider's commands. The rider was supposed to be tall in the saddle, quiet, focused. Then why, Lisa wondered, did it feel as if every time Prancer went up, she went down? Why did Prancer stiffen through the corners as if she might tip over? Why did Lisa's outside leg feel weak and her inside leg feel numb? Why couldn't they look like the horses and riders in the textbooks on dressage? Every time Lisa passed the mirrors on the long side of the indoor ring, she cringed. She sneaked a glance at the rest of the class to see how her peers were faring.

Stevie and Carole didn't seem to be doing much better. Belle was tossing her head—a sign of protest and impatience, not harmony. Starlight was prancing along. He looked as if he were overflowing with energy. Every so often he would shy at an imaginary ghost. Simon Atherton, on Barq, looked stiff and heavy-handed. The Arab was walking at a graveyard pace, leaning on the reins.

15

Andrea Barry, riding her horse, Doc, had a pained, irritated expression on her face. After a moment Lisa guessed why: The girl's boots looked brand new. They were probably a Christmas present she was breaking in—and if they were as tight as they looked, they were pinching her hard, making it impossible to use her legs properly. Finally Lisa focused on Veronica diAngelo. To Lisa's annoyance, the snobbish girl looked relaxed and confident. Danny, Veronica's top-dollar show horse, was walking happily along with a spring in his step. Veronica's tanned face told the story: The diAngelos had taken one of their deluxe vacations, leaving stable hand Red O'Malley to exercise Danny. Whenever the diAngelos went away they paid extra to have the expensive horse exercised. Red was an excellent rider, so Veronica always came home to a well-schooled horse.

"Not bad, Veronica," called Max from the center of the ring. "You've got him walking nicely on the bit."

"He means, 'Not bad, *Red*,' " grumbled Stevie as Belle caught up to Prancer.

Lisa flashed a grin at her friend. At least with The Saddle Club, she thought, you always saw the lighter side of things.

"All right, everyone pick up a trot—a sitting trot," Max commanded.

Lisa saw Stevie grimace. Rising or posting to the trot

16

was much easier. Sitting could be jarring and uncomfortable.

"Could it get any worse?" Stevie muttered, shortening her reins. "I'm sore already, from the warm-up."

"At least we're not riding without stirrups," Lisa whispered.

As if he had heard her, Max looked right at the two of them and said, "No, wait a minute. First everyone drop his or her stirrups. *Then* pick up a sitting trot."

Lisa and Stevie groaned in unison before doing what they'd been told.

Across the ring Carole murmured, "Darn! Darn, darn, darn!" This just wasn't her day. She had been so busy reading *Horseman's Weekly* that she had completely forgotten about giving Starlight a prelesson warm-up. Now he was paying her back by spooking at every shadow and speck of dirt. Steeling herself, Carole took her feet out of the stirrups, which she crossed over Starlight's neck. Sure enough, the minute she picked up a trot, he got faster and faster, as if to say, "I hate dressage! When can we jump?"

"Have you been longeing him, Carole?" Max called.

Carole had no choice but to shake her head. "I—I haven't had time," she said, though she knew it was a lame excuse.

"Make time, Carole," Max said sternly. "You know how fit he is. You've got to take the edge off."

Carole said nothing, only nodded. The sole response she could have made was: "I know! I know!" As she rounded the corner of the ring near the stalls, Starlight plunged forward and gave a small buck. All at once Carole was fed up. Outwardly she remained calm; she was far too good a horsewoman to take out her frustration on her horse. She straightened him out and brought him back to a steady trot. But inwardly she wished she were mounted on a horse who *liked* these drills, who liked dressage, who didn't need eight jumps in front of him to get down to work . . .

"Lisa, your seat belongs in the saddle, not on Prancer's neck. Simon, tighten your reins, they're flopping all over the place. Stevie—*Stevie!*" Max sounded irate. "Did you hear me say *drop* your stirrups?"

"Yes," came Stevie's faint reply.

"Then why are your feet in yours?" Max demanded.

"Because my legs are killing me!" exclaimed Stevie, to the delight of the rest of the class.

"After five minutes?" Max asked doubtfully.

"Yes! Belle's trot is so bouncy! Couldn't we canter?"

"Blame your own fitness, Stevie, not your horse's gait."

"But Max," Stevie pleaded, "five minutes on her is like . . . half an hour on another horse!"

"Well, then, I suppose half an hour is like three hours. You can let me know if I'm right at the end of the lesson,"

18

Max added, a glint in his eye. As Stevie moaned, Max dragged a few trotting poles into place and laid them on the ground. "All right. Starting with Simon, assume jumping position, turn down the center line, and trot over the poles."

AT THE END of the lesson, Max summoned the riders into the center of the ring. "There now, that wasn't so bad, was it?"

"I'll never walk again," Stevie muttered.

"Any questions?"

Simon Atherton put up a hand.

"Yes?"

"Why did we use trotting poles in a dressage lesson?" Simon asked. "I thought they were for warming up before jumping."

"Good question. Who can answer it?"

Several hands were raised.

"They're good for lengthening and shortening stride," Andrea said.

"Right. Who else?"

"They make the horses pick up their feet?" Lisa guessed.

"Ye-es, okay: They make the horses pay attention and move more alertly," said Max. "Anyone else? Carole?"

Carole looked up from Starlight's mane. "What?

Sorry?" Brooding over her and Starlight's poor performance, she had missed the question.

Max repeated it. "Give us a very basic answer."

"Hmmm . . . I guess they would make the lesson more interesting?" Carole ventured.

"That's right. It's very important to vary your schooling routine," Max explained. "You shouldn't just get on every day, walk, trot, canter, two cross rails, that's that. Horses are like people: They get bored if they do the same thing over and over, just the way you would. I'm mentioning it now because it's more of a problem in winter than in summer. In winter you're riding indoors more, taking fewer trail rides, going to fewer competitions. Horses can get barn fever, which can make them cranky and stubborn. By throwing in a few surprises, like trotting poles in a dressage lesson, you can liven things up."

"Is that what torturing your students does?" Stevie moaned. "Livens things up?"

"What? By riding without stirrups?" Max grinned. "No, that *toughens* things up—namely, your legs and seat. I can't have Pine Hollow turning into a bunch of couch potatoes just because it's January!"

"Couch potatoes!" Stevie wailed. "I feel more like *mashed* potatoes!"

"Well, Stevie, you'll have plenty of time to recover. First of all, I want everyone to take tomorrow off. It's

Sunday. Give yourselves a rest. And secondly, I have an announcement to make: This will be your last lesson for two weeks." Max paused, looking slightly sheepish at the murmurs that followed. "No, I'm not going off to hunt in Ireland or teach clinics in England or judge an international Pony Club competition. I won't be anywhere near horses for two weeks. I'm, uh, going on vacation."

There was a spontaneous burst of applause from the group. Like many horse people, Max Regnery *never* went on vacation—except to take a busman's holiday.

"Who talked you into it, Max?" Lisa inquired, though she had a pretty good idea of the answer.

"Deborah," Max replied, as Lisa had thought he would. "Naturally."

"Do you need a baby-sitter?" Stevie asked.

Max smiled. "No, but thanks for asking. We're taking Maxi with us. We're going up to Vermont to visit Deborah's parents. The Hales would never speak to us again if we left their granddaughter with a sitter."

Maxi was the Regnerys' baby girl. The Saddle Club had been there when she was born, and they had taken her on her first horseback ride. Sometimes they felt like Maxi's aunts.

"But," Max continued, "getting back to the two weeks I'll be away, I expect you all to work very hard. Your next lesson will be the Saturday after next." He paused and seemed to be thinking. The Saddle Club waited nervously. The words *work very hard* followed by a silence could mean only one thing: Max was devising a scheme to *ensure* that they worked very hard. A moment later he spoke up again. "I want you all to work very hard," he repeated. "So why doesn't everyone plan on *demonstrating* what he or she has worked on? Instead of your usual lesson, I'll expect a performance of sorts from each of you. It will be a little test to see how you do without supervision."

Stevie, Lisa, and Carole exchanged glances. They weren't fooled for a minute by that word *little*. Max would expect real progress.

"Max?" Veronica said. "I'm afraid my performance will have to be on the slopes. You see," she added with a giggle, "I'm going skiing out West for the next ten days."

"I thought you already went on vacation!" Stevie blurted out indignantly.

Veronica smiled sweetly. "I already went on vacation to the Caribbean. I haven't taken my ski holiday yet."

"Yes, well, you'll have to do the best you can, Veronica," Max said shortly.

"All right, Max, I'll try my hardest," she promised.

"Is Red going to be in charge?" Carole inquired, ignoring the gagging noises Stevie was directing at Veronica.

"Yes—Red and my mother. Stevie," Max asked, "is something the matter?"

"Oh, no, Max. I was just wishing Veronica a great trip." The change in Stevie's expression from disgust to innocence was so fast that Carole and Lisa had trouble keeping straight faces. "You have a great trip, too, Max," Stevie added.

"Thanks," Max said dryly. "I will."

AFTER THE LESSON, Lisa untacked in a hurry. She gave Prancer the barest brushing. There was no time to put polish on the mare's hooves, practice braiding her forelock, or go for that extra shine with the stable rag. She was barely going to make her hair appointment as it was. "Sorry, Prancer," she murmured. "I promise I'll make it up to you." She closed the door of Prancer's stall and latched it.

"Want to help me sweep the tack room?" Carole asked as the girls hung up their saddles and bridles.

"Uh, I can't today, Carole," Lisa said. "My mom's waiting. I have to get a haircut."

"Oh. Okay," said Carole.

"Where? Cosmo Cuts?" Stevie asked.

Lisa nodded. "It was the only time Charles could fit me in."

"Sure, I'll bet. You just want to get out of sweeping the tack room," Stevie teased.

"That's not true!" Lisa said hotly. "I always help out!"

Stevie looked at her friend, her eyebrows raised. "Jeez, what is it today? Nobody can take a joke!"

"Oh," said Lisa, embarrassed. "Sorry. Anyway, I guess I'll—I'll see you guys tomorrow."

"Monday, you mean," Carole corrected her. "We have tomorrow off."

"That's right!" Lisa exclaimed. Embarrassed for a second time, she realized how enthusiastic she sounded. "I mean, you know, that's, uh, right."

"Enjoy the pampering," Stevie murmured after her.

Lisa hurried out to the driveway. Her mother's gray sedan was waiting. As Lisa slid into the passenger side she heard someone call, "Bye, Lisa!" She craned her neck to see who it was. Veronica diAngelo was getting into the next car over—a chauffeured white Mercedes. "Leaving early, huh, Lisa?" Veronica said pointedly.

Annoyed, Lisa nodded. "Yeah. Haircut," she said, giving a brief wave as they drove off. It was one thing to have Carole and Stevie know she had left right after the lesson. It was another to be caught by Veronica.

"Wasn't that that nice diAngelo girl?" asked Mrs. Atwood. "I do wish you would invite her to sleep over sometime, Lisa. Her family is *so* well connected. . . ."

STEVIE KNEW AN opportunity when she saw one. She sank down onto a tack trunk, yanked off her boots, and wiggled her toes. "Phew, what a lesson. I'm exhausted," she said. She eyed Carole narrowly. "How are you feeling?"

"Fine," Carole said. "Why?"

"Oh, I don't know. . . . I was just thinking that, you know, I've got some laundry to do at home. And with Lisa gone, we're going to be a lot less efficient. So maybe we ought to, oh, say . . ."

"Skip the barn work entirely?" Carole guessed, her black eyes sparkling.

Stevie grinned. Unlike Lisa, Stevie didn't mind being accused of ducking out on stable chores. It was a well-known fact that Stevie despised barn work. She didn't really *hate* it, but work was work. And no work was the best work. She would have ducked out every day if she could! "Now, Carole, I know what you're thinking, but—"

Carole was about to argue Stevie into staying when she caught sight of the *Horseman's Weekly* crushed under her friend's right ankle. A curious instinct seemed to take

26

over. She heard herself saying, in a falsely bright voice, "Hey, we don't have to hang out every single day. It's vacation! We should enjoy ourselves."

Surprised, Stevie sat up. "Now you're talking!" she said. "So you'll head out with me?"

"Oh, no," Carole replied. "I can't. I've got to work with Starlight and organize my tack trunk and put my brushes in order and—"

"All right, all right, you're making me feel guilty!" Stevie protested.

"Don't," said Carole. "I mean, I want to stay awhile, but you do what you need to do."

Disconcerted, Stevie put her boots back on. She'd been all ready to bargain with Carole, but Carole was letting her off the hook completely.

"All right—well, bye," Stevie said when she was ready.

"Bye! Have fun!" Carole said.

"Thanks," Stevie said flatly. For the second time that day she found herself face-to-face with Carole's constant and total devotion to Starlight. And for the second time she found it annoying. Couldn't Carole ever think of anything else?

On the way out Stevie passed Belle's stall. She paused to say good-bye. She told herself she was just as devoted to Belle, but in a different way. "If you were a human, you wouldn't want to clean tack, either," she rationalized, rubbing the mare's forehead. "Would you, you Southern Belle?

"Whoops, I better skedaddle!" she said, hearing Mrs. Reg coming down the aisle. Before the older woman could catch her idle, Stevie had jogged out of the barn and down the driveway. But after fifty yards she was forced to slow to a walk—actually more like a pained shuffle. Hobbling home, she chewed on a thumbnail. Could it be true what Alex had said about her level of physical fitness? "Ha!" she said aloud. "Let him try riding without stirrups!"

WHENEVER CAROLE ATE a piece of cake, she ate the cake first and saved the frosting for last. It was a habit she'd had for as long as she could remember. Sometimes it applied to other things, like what she did that day: As soon as Stevie left, Carole snatched up *Horseman's Weekly* and turned right to the advertisements. But before letting herself study the ad Stevie had noticed, she reread some of the others. Then, making sure she was still alone, she slowly savored the "frosting."

16.2 hand, 8-year-old Dutch warmblood. Experienced, high-level dressage horse. Big, floating trot, excellent extensions. Imported from Holland three years ago. Has won major dressage competitions, both locally and nationally. King's Ransom is ready to go all the way with the right rider.

Carole looked up. She could almost see the horse's "big, floating trot." The phrase *the right rider* sent a shiver down her spine. What exactly did it mean? Did it mean an Olympic-level dressage rider? Or maybe a young rider with a lot of potential? Carole read the ad once more. Warmbloods, as she knew, were wonderful horses. Bigger and steadier than Thoroughbreds, they were bred for dressage and eventing, whereas Thoroughbreds were bred for racing. Originally from Europe, many types of warmbloods were now bred in the United States. Still, a horse that was imported had a certain allure, almost as if it were more authentic. It was one of Carole's wildest dreams to be able to import a horse of her own. As she pictured herself in Holland or Germany, touring the national studs, the door opened and a woman came in.

"So *you've* got the *Horseman's Weekly*," she said.

Carole looked up. "Yeah, I was just reading about the annual writing contest," she lied, wondering, as she did so, why she would bother to fib to a stranger. "Did you want the paper?"

"I'll have a look at the ads, if you don't mind. But go ahead, tear out the page for the contest."

"That's okay. I'll—I'll just copy down the rules later." Hastily Carole handed over the paper.

"Thanks. I'm Pat Naughton, by the way," said the woman, extending a hand.

Carole shook it. "Carole—"

"Oh, I know who you are, Carole."

"You do?" said Carole. On closer look she thought she recognized the woman as well.

"Of course. You own Starlight. You and he are one of the top junior teams at Pine Hollow. You've won everything—Pony Club, dressage, eventing, jumping—"

"Mostly jumping," Carole broke in, flattered and flustered at the same time. "Jumping is our favorite and it's what we're best at."

Pat Naughton beamed. "I'll say. I've watched you two in lessons. Starlight's fantastic over fences."

"He's a great natural jumper—" Carole began.

"Who had a great trainer," Pat finished for her. "But you sure are lucky. If I had a horse even half as perfect as Starlight, I wouldn't have to spend my days scouring the ads." She tapped the newspaper. "Anything good this week?"

"What are you looking for?" Carole inquired politely.

"That's what I keep asking myself!" said Pat. "May I?"

She sat down beside Carole. "You see, I haven't owned a horse since I was your age. I just got back into riding a year ago, when my daughter started kindergarten. I used to show. I rode hunters, jumpers, equitation—you name it. But this dressage stuff is pretty new to me."

Carole nodded understandingly. "I'll bet you were doing dressage before without even knowing it."

"Really?" said Pat. "All this 'on the bit' stuff?"

Carole laughed. "Sure. All that means is that the horse is moving forward from the leg and accepting rather than resisting the bit."

Pat looked impressed. "Wow."

Feeling shy, Carole averted her eyes. She was used to grown-ups being surprised at the information that would come popping out of her mouth, making her sound much older than she was. "It—It sounds like you want a good all-around horse," she suggested, looking up again. "And probably something . . . experienced?"

"Definitely!" Pat exclaimed. "I've got a daughter at home. I don't need a green horse to raise at the same time."

Slowly, with a few knowledgeable questions, Carole managed to piece together an idea of what Pat wanted in her new horse. Horse shopping was not a precise science. A rider couldn't expect to go out and find her dream horse, especially since a lot of the ads would exaggerate the pluses and downplay the horse's faults. But it was good to at least have an idea of what characteristics—age, experience, and breed, for example—were most important. Some riders had little idiosyncrasies, like a favorite color, but Pat's requirements were fairly straightforward. Besides experience, she needed a large horse because she was tall. Because of her daughter, she wanted something quiet-tempered. "It doesn't seem as if it would be that hard," Pat confessed, "but I've been looking for over a month with no luck."

"Let's take a look," suggested Carole, her enthusiasm for the project mounting. "You never know. This could be your lucky week."

Together she and Pat pored over the advertisements. Pat had a pencil, and whenever she saw something she liked, she marked it. Pretty soon Carole had Pat's system figured out: A star meant "sounds great," a circle meant "worth looking into," and a squiggle meant "probably not but might as well give them a call." The "seasoned hunter" got a star. The "superbly talented four-year-old" got a squiggle. Then Pat poised her pencil above the Dutch warmblood. Carole felt her stomach turn with apprehension.

"Gosh, this warmblood sounds like a beauty," Pat remarked.

"He sure does," Carole said quietly.

Pat chewed the end of her pencil. "Hmmm . . . 'Imported,' it says. 'King's Ransom' . . . *Costs* a king's ransom, I'll bet!"

"Gosh, I never thought of price," Carole admitted, her face falling.

"Heck, why should you? You're not looking yourself," said Pat.

"Oh, I know," Carole said hastily. "I mean—I never thought of price for you."

"Don't worry," Pat joked. "My husband will think plenty." Her eyes scanned the page. "No price listed on the warmblood. Naturally. They never put the price when they're asking a bundle. Well, we'll give it a circle, anyway."

Carole didn't stop to analyze why, but she was glad—glad that the warmblood got a circle instead of a star.

WHENEVER STEVIE MADE cookies, half the batter ended up in her stomach. For her, half the *point* of making cookies was eating the batter. If you just wanted cookies, you could go to the store. Today she was making her favorite kind: oatmeal chocolate chip. Most people made oatmeal raisin, but Stevie knew better. In the first place, she detested raisins. Who wanted those icky, dried, chewy things in their cookies? If you wanted fruit, you could eat an apple! But straight chocolate chip cookies were almost too sweet. After a few you just couldn't take the sugar. Better to moderate the sugar taste with something grainy like oatmeal. Adding oatmeal had two other advantages: One, it made the cookie sound healthful/nutritionally sound/after-school-snack-acceptable, which meant her mother would let her eat a lot more than if she thought they were a plain old tooth-rotting dessert. And two, the batter was the best!

"Wanna lick the bowl?" Stevie asked Alex as he tore through the kitchen.

Alex stopped dead. He drew himself up to his full height and gave his sister an appalled look. "Did I hear you correctly? Are you suggesting that I eat raw cookie dough?"

"It *is* your favorite dessert," Stevie reminded him, annoyed. She wasn't going to let him get away with this health nut act.

"*Was* my favorite dessert!" Alex retorted. "Before I saw the light! Before I began representing Fenton Hall in athletic competitions! Before I reduced my body mass index to a mere—"

Alex ducked as Stevie chucked a wooden spoon at him.

"Perhaps," he continued, righting himself, "if you found a physical outlet for your rage, sister dear, you wouldn't feel compelled—"

"I'll take up strangling!" Stevie growled, chasing him out of the kitchen.

"Maybe you'd have a prayer of catching me if you did more than sit around baking all day!" Alex taunted.

Back in the kitchen, Stevie asked, "Mom, do you think I'm out of shape?"

Mrs. Lake looked up from stirring her sauce. "Don't you have required sports at school?" she asked.

"Yeah, but I got out of sports this semester to be in a play," Stevie said.

"A play?" Mrs. Lake looked surprised.

"Yeah," said Stevie. "But then I didn't get the part, so I got out of the play to do special choir."

"Oh." Frowning, Mrs. Lake stared at the sauce. "Wait. Did you say *choir?*"

"C'mon, Mom, I have been taking voice lessons. Anyway, I got out of it," Stevie assured her. "To do sports."

"So you do get exercise at school?" asked Mrs. Lake, exasperated.

Stevie shook her head. "No, I don't. Remember, Mom? I said I got *out* of sports."

Mrs. Lake raised her eyes to the heavens. "When's the last time you got any exercise?"

Stevie opened the oven door and put two cookie sheets in to bake. "Well . . . I just scooped a bunch of cookies," she said hopefully.

"No, Stevie, I mean *real* exercise."

"Does riding count?"

"I don't know. Does it?"

Stevie thought for a moment. She tried to be honest with herself. In a way she understood why riding got such a bad rap. Riding was one of those weird sports. It required a lot of different muscles; it required stamina. Anybody who tried it would ache for days afterward. But even if somebody rode every day for an hour, she wouldn't be in shape to run five miles. Or even, necessarily, two miles. Sort of," Stevie said finally.

Mrs. Lake raised an eyebrow at her daughter. She was a high-powered attorney in Washington, D.C., and this was her high-powered-attorney look. Stevie knew that look well. It said: Until you make up your mind, I can be of no further help to you.

"I'll think about it, Mom," Stevie amended.

"Good," said the attorney. "Now pass over that bowl for me to lick."

"ALL RIGHT," SAID Pat Naughton, "then I'll see you Monday at ten." She snapped her cellular phone closed and flopped down onto a bench next to Carole. "Gosh, you'd think these people didn't *want* to sell their horses, the way they fuss about setting up appointments."

"Maybe they're afraid the horses won't look right in a certain light," Carole joked. She had cleaned and oiled her tack but was lingering to talk with Pat. Pat seemed to like having her there. Every time the woman made an appointment to look at a horse, she would ask Carole if she thought the horse was worth seeing.

"It wouldn't surprise me," Pat said. "I've been looking so long that *nothing* surprises me."

"Have you seen anything good?" Carole asked.

Pat nodded. "There's a mare in Pleasantville I like a lot, but she's a little old—fifteen. I'd be worried about her slowing down in a few years. You know," she added, tapping one of the ads she had marked, "I don't know about this gelding. I gave him a star, but he almost sounds too quiet. The owner kept emphasizing what a great *beginner* horse he'd make."

"Hmmm," Carole mused. "That could mean safe and reliable. On the other hand, it could mean that he has trouble getting out of a trot. You just never know till you see them, do you?"

"Nope," agreed Pat. She ran a manicured hand through her blond hair. Carole noticed that she wore a large diamond ring and an expensive-looking watch. Some people—most people—Carole would have criticized for wearing jewelry in the barn. But Pat was so nice and friendly that Carole found herself admiring the woman's style. It was kind of horsey chic. And her enthusiasm was catching.

"I keep trying to explain that to my husband. He says, 'Why don't you just pick one!' He grew up in the city, so he can't help it." Pat laughed. "He knows as much about horses as I do about the stock market. *Nada!*"

"My dad was the same way," Carole said, giggling at the memory. "Don't worry—he'll get better once you actually own a horse."

"I hope so," said Pat. "I just wish I had someone to consult, to take with me on these horse-shopping excursions. If Max were around . . . But he's too busy, anyway." She glanced at her watch. "Well, I'd better make this last call and then get going. My baby-sitter's probably run away by now."

"Um . . . Pat?" Carole said quickly. "I'd go with you to look at horses. I mean," she added, feeling shy, "if you think it would help."

"Help? Are you kidding? It would be great!" Pat said. "Are you sure you have the time?"

"Sure," said Carole. "I'm on vacation."

"Well, fabulous! I've got appointments all Monday morning."

"All morning? That's fine. That's perfect," said Carole, thinking fast. She could go with Pat in the morning, then ride Starlight in the afternoon.

"Gosh, this is wonderful. I'll feel so much better with

you there. Okay: last call." Pat whipped out her cellular phone again and dialed a number. "Yes, I'm calling about King's Ransom. . . ."

Carole felt herself stiffen.

"Uh-huh. . . . How about Monday afternoon? About three? Great. . . . No, I'm not a beginner, but until last year I hadn't ridden seriously since I was fifteen. . . . Yes, yes, I love dressage." Pat rolled her eyes as she answered several more questions. Carole listened attentively, wondering what could be taking so long.

"That's a new one!" Pat exclaimed when the call had ended. "The owner was interviewing *me*."

"Really?" said Carole.

"Yes—to see if I'd be a worthy purchaser for her amazing horse! I'll bet it's just another selling technique." Shaking her head, Pat stood up. She reached into her handbag and pulled out a key chain. "Say, do you need a ride somewhere? I've got my car outside."

Carole accepted happily. She followed Pat out to the driveway. It was strange: She couldn't decide whether or not she was glad they were going to see King. (In her head she had already nicknamed King's Ransom.) Part of her wished he would stay an advertisement in *Horseman's Weekly*, but part of her was excited at the chance to see a horse like that up close. *Maybe he'll be too expensive or Pat won't like him*, she thought. *And then* . . . But there was no ending to that thought. And as she climbed into Pat's sports car, Carole had to admit that despite what she had said, her new friend probably had the money to buy any horse she liked.

"I just realized something," Pat remarked, backing out of the parking space. "I made the last appointment for three in the afternoon. Is that going to be too long a day for you?"

"Oh, no," Carole said hastily. "It's fine."

"Are you sure?" Pat said. "Because if you want, I could drop you off after the morning round and then go see this King's Ransom myself."

"No, really," Carole insisted, "I'll come along." Mentally she rescheduled the afternoon. If she got back at five, she could still take a quick ride. Then again, she thought, it wasn't as if there were a *law* about riding every day. . . .

STEVIE GROANED, THREW back the covers, and got out of bed: Monday, 9:00 A.M. No more pretending she didn't hear that alarm ringing. Today she was turning over a new leaf. She had spent Sunday lying in bed. Today she was going to get to Pine Hollow early and get it over with. Groom, ride, groom, and be back home by noon. Then she could spend the afternoon doing what she wanted to do: baking, watching TV, lying on the sofa half-asleep—in other words, enjoying vacation.

As she dressed she looked absently at a framed picture of her, Lisa, and Carole on their horses. It had been taken a long time ago. Stevie could tell the picture was old, not just because it had been on her wall forever, but because of the horse each girl was riding. Lisa was on Pepper, a flea-bitten speckled gray that had taught her everything she knew before he'd had to be put down. Carole was on another of Max's school horses, Barq, the chestnut Arabian, her sometime mount in the days before Starlight. And Stevie was riding Topside, a bay Thoroughbred she had ridden and taken to lots of shows at the time. Mrs. Reg had taken the picture to use up some film and had made a copy for each of the girls. Normally Stevie smiled at the sight of the picture. But today she felt as if it were watching her somehow. "I just hope you guys don't force me to hang out all afternoon," she muttered to her friends in the photograph. "I've got a vacation to enjoy!"

It wasn't until Stevie was across the room and halfway into her jeans that she did a complete double take. She glanced behind her at the picture, afraid that Carole or Lisa had overheard her thoughts. She wanted to go to Pine Hollow to "get it over with"? She wanted to spend the afternoon "enjoying" vacation? Since when had riding become a dreaded task? Since when had it ceased being her absolute favorite thing in the whole wide world? Stevie hardly knew what to think. Better not to think at all, she decided. Better to go ride and see if she felt different when she got there. Of course she would feel different! One look at Belle and—and—and she would realize how badly Belle's mane needed pulling, Stevie

43

thought glumly. With a sigh, she slipped a sweater over her long-sleeved T-shirt. She looked out the window. It was gray out. Again. Just like her mood. Sometimes she wished her family lived in New England instead of Virginia, or out West like the Devines—or anywhere that got a real winter. "What's the point of winter if you don't get huge snowstorms?" she grumbled, pulling her hair back with an elastic. Unfortunately, snow made her think of Max. Max was in Vermont. Max would be back from Vermont in two weeks, expecting progress, gray days or not.

"Or Florida! Or California! Why can't we live in California?" Stevie muttered, pushing open the kitchen door.

Chad and Michael, seated at the kitchen table, wrinkled their noses. "Ugh: horse," Michael said, sniffing loudly.

"It wouldn't be that bad if she washed her clothes more than twice a year," Chad said.

Stevie shot him a withering glance. "I wouldn't want to go near your gym bag, either," she retorted.

"Mine?" Chad cried. "Mine's nothing compared to Alex's!"

"Yeah, Stevie," said Michael, grinning. "You've got competition in the body odor department now."

Before Stevie could decide whether that was a compliment or an insult, her "competition" strode through the door, clad in spandex running tights. "Loading up on carbohydrates again?" said Alex, giving the breakfast table a disapproving glance.

"What, you don't eat toast and cereal anymore?" Chad asked.

Alex seemed to recoil at the notion. "Not before twelve! My Power-Fitness shake gives me all the protein I need for my morning run," he bragged.

"Great," said Stevie, scowling at her twin. "Then why don't you take that run?"

"Yeah, like *now*," added Chad. "And leave the rest of us to eat breakfast in peace!"

"Amen!" said Michael.

Stevie felt her scowl fading. Three against one was typical in the Lake household, but she was usually the one, not one of the three! Evidently Alex's fitness regime was getting to Chad and Michael, too.

Alex ignored the comments. He put a hand on his hip and stretched out his right side. "Sure nobody wants to join me?" he asked. "Just a quick three? Down to the dirt road and back? Chad? Michael? No takers?"

"What about me?" Stevie demanded. "How do you know I don't want to go running with you?"

Alex gave her a condescending smile. "One, I can see—I mean *smell*—that you're ready to go riding. And two, I'm sorry, Stevie, but I'm going running, not jogging and breaking to a walk every five minutes. I've got a training schedule to keep to."

Chad nodded solicitously. "He's got a point, Stevie. With all that baking you've been doing, you've put on a pound or two. You might have trouble on the hills."

Stevie glared at her older brother. How dare he change sides on her! "You're not exactly ready for the marathon, Chad!" she snapped.

Chad shrugged. "Who said I was?"

"Yeah, who said he was?" Michael echoed.

"Copycat!" Stevie spun around to face Alex, her face aflame. "Are you saying I couldn't keep up with you?"

" 'Fraid so," said Alex, stretching out his other side.

"No, I mean, are you *saying* I couldn't keep up with you?" Stevie demanded.

"*Oh*," said Alex with understanding. "You mean am I *daring* you to *try* to keep up with me?"

"That's right," Stevie said through gritted teeth.

Alex beamed. "Well, yes. I guess I am."

Stevie felt herself blanch, but just for an instant. "All right," she said, her voice perfectly calm. "Then I'll just have to prove you wrong."

"I'm leaving in two minutes!" Alex called as Stevie ran up the stairs. She went to the laundry pile and dug out a pair of sweats. In two minutes she was back downstairs, waiting at the front door.

46

"Aren't you going to stretch out?" Alex asked, aghast.

"Stretching is for wimps," she said disdainfully.

"We-ell, all right. Any time you're ready, then," Alex said.

"After you," said Stevie, opening the door.

Outside, Alex paused to look at her. "You're really going to run the whole way without stopping?" he asked. "Three miles?"

"Oh, is it only three miles? Such a shame." Stevie shook her head ruefully. "And I was hoping for a real workout. I guess I'll have to get that later—when I go riding."

"Ha, ha, ha, ha, ha. Riding! All you do is sit there! The horse does all the work!"

Stevie stretched out her hands to throttle her brother, but it was too late. He had already sprinted down the driveway. Swearing revenge, Stevie started after him. She had run down the driveway hundreds, thousands of times. But somehow it had never seemed so long.

LISA WAS WHISTLING at her work. She'd had a productive day off, she'd gotten a good night's sleep, she'd read a few chapters of *To Kill a Mockingbird* that morning—already— and she *loved* her new haircut. Rising halfway from her desk, she turned her head this way and that in the mirror. Her shiny, light brown locks swung from side to side, just above her shoulders. Vacation was great. It was so nice to catch up on all the things she needed to do. Even writing the thank-you notes wasn't so bad.

Dear Mrs. Chambers, Lisa wrote. *Thank you for the needlepoint kit.* She paused, chewing on the end of her pen. The problem with thank-you notes was that after you said thank you there was nothing else to say. *I love the horsey theme. It's so "me."* Ugh. Now she was really stuck. And she still had three quarters of the page to fill. There was only one solution, one that Stevie had suggested as her method of dealing with lame adult gifts: lie outright. Lisa smiled. *I love needlepoint. I find it a relaxing pastime, and I can't wait to start this particular pattern.* Feeling very Stevie-ish, Lisa signed the card with a flourish, sealed and addressed the envelope, and sat back in her chair.

It was nine-thirty in the morning. Probably time to think about getting a ride over to Pine Hollow. On Lisa's desk was a framed picture of The Saddle Club—of her, Carole, and Stevie with the horses they had ridden when they were first friends, the horses that in a way had brought them together. Lisa loved that picture. It reminded her of the two Saddle Club rules, that everyone had to be horse-crazy and had to be willing to help each other out in any situation. "Too bad needlepoint doesn't count as a situation," Lisa mused aloud. She opened her top desk drawer and took out the needlepoint kit. It really was a nice pattern. It would make a good pillow covering—maybe as a gift for little Maxi.

As Lisa stood up from her desk, she caught sight of herself in the mirror again. She frowned. It was silly, but she wasn't looking forward to wrecking her new haircut by crushing it under a hard hat and getting all sweaty. She could wash it later, but it wouldn't look as good. As she was debating what to do, there was a knock on the door and her mother walked into the room. "I'm heading out to run some errands, dear. Do you want to come?" said Mrs. Atwood.

"Where are you going?" Lisa inquired.

"Post office, dry cleaner's, but mainly the library. I've got to return some books, and your dad wants a new mystery."

Lisa chewed her lip. She loved going to the library. She liked to settle into the reading room while her mother browsed the adult section. But Stevie and Carole were probably already at the barn. After their day off, they'd be raring to go. They would also be wondering where she was.

"It'll be fun," Mrs. Atwood urged. "We can stop at Tastee Delight on the way home."

"TD's?" Lisa said. It was the town's ice cream parlor. She, Stevie, and Carole often went there after riding.

49

"Yes, I'm going to break my diet and have a sundae."

"I'm supposed to go to Pine Hollow," Lisa said reluctantly.

"What time are you meeting the girls?" asked her mother, for once not harping on the amount of time Lisa spent there.

"We didn't set a time," Lisa answered. "But usually everyone gets there around now. Max is away, you see, and we're supposed to be working extra hard—"

Now Mrs. Atwood did interrupt, frowning ever so slightly. "Does it ever occur to that man that there might be other things you have to work on? I mean, other things besides walk, trot, and canter?"

Lisa smiled in spite of herself. "Max gave us a day off—yesterday. It's just Prancer. I don't want to let her down."

"Prancer's a *horse*," said Mrs. Atwood, the way only a nonhorsey person could. "Another day off isn't going to *kill* her, for heaven's sakes."

Lisa had to admit that her mother had a point. That was the thing about nonhorsey people. They didn't understand at all, but sometimes they were right. "You know what, Mom? I will come with you. I can go riding this afternoon." Out of the corner of her eye, Lisa could see the picture of The Saddle Club on her desk. She felt a twinge of guilt. "Stevie and Carole will just have to get along without me," she said aloud.

"That's right. As I always say, you don't have to spend every waking hour there." Mrs. Atwood turned briskly and left the room.

Lisa tidied up her desk, brushed her hair for the millionth time, and went downstairs. She had a strange feeling. She couldn't place it until she realized it was relief: She was relieved that she was not going to the barn. "Big deal," she said aloud. Morning or afternoon—it made no difference when she rode. Except that she wasn't all that psyched for afternoon, either.

"Bring your riding clothes if you want, Lisa," Mrs. Atwood suggested. "And I can drop you off on the way home."

Lisa hesitated. She had pictured herself coming home and lying on the family room couch with a large stack of new books to read. And, oddly enough, she was kind of looking forward to starting the needlepoint. "Umm . . . That's okay," she said. "I don't want to make you wait."

"It's no trouble, sweetheart. Why don't you run up and get your breeches?"

"No, really," Lisa said more firmly. "I don't know if I'm even going to ride at all today. I thought about it and you're right, Mom: Two days off isn't going to make a difference."

Lisa's mother gave her a funny look. "Are you feeling all right, Lisa?"

51

"Yes, I'm fine, Mom! I don't have to hang out there twenty-four/seven, do I?"

"No, dear," said Mrs. Atwood, "you certainly don't. But let me just take your temperature anyway. I can't remember the last time you skipped riding voluntarily."

STEVIE'S FACE WAS burning up. It was January and she was so hot she wanted to jump into a bathtub of ice. Her ankles were wobbling. She couldn't feel her right foot. Her stomach felt like lead. Her lips were parched. She wanted to retch. Gasping for air, she turned the last corner before home. Up ahead she could make out a figure— barely. The figure was charging up the driveway like a gazelle. Stevie looked down at the road. She watched her feet hitting the pavement. She had no idea what or who was picking them up and putting them down again. It certainly wasn't her. She looked back up the driveway. The figure was doing a dance. An odd tribal victory dance of some kind. *I. Will. Not. Stop. I. Will. Not. Stop*, Stevie chanted in her head. The figure had stopped dancing and was running—running toward her.

"Hey! Stevie! I'll run the last fifty with you. How you feeling, huh? You look like you're lagging a little. You want to pick up the right foot, not drag it like that. Come on, sis!"

Stevie looked at Alex. She couldn't speak; she didn't

have the breath. But mentally she said, *You are going to die a horrible death inflicted by me.* To herself she chanted, *I. Will. Not. Stop.* Then all of a sudden she did. She just stopped. Then she walked, at an aching shuffle, holding her side, panting, tasting the acrid flavor of defeat.

"Aw, too bad. You were *so close*," Alex said. He gave Stevie a whack on the back. "Better luck next time," he said, sprinting toward the house.

"Rematch!" Stevie yelled after him. Or tried to yell. The words came out in a whisper. "Rematch!" she murmured hoarsely. "I demand a rematch!"

A FEW MINUTES later, Stevie was stretched out on the couch, a cold cloth pressed to her head, a pitcher of ice water balanced on her lap. She had never felt so awful in her entire life. Then Alex came in. "You should never lie down after exercising," he said. "You've got to bring the heart rate down slowly." He proceeded to do a series of jumping jacks and squat thrusts in front of her.

Stevie didn't trust herself to engage in conversation, but there was one point that had to be made. "Rematch," she said, staring stonily at the ceiling.

Alex paused midsquat. "What was that?"

"Rematch," Stevie repeated, her voice steely.

"You want a rematch? I don't know. It would be so boring. Well, maybe if we tested, like, overall fitness—

53

strength, endurance, et cetera. I'd still whip you, but at least there'd be something interesting about it."

"One week," Stevie said.

"One week? I'd better give you two to try to get into something resembling fitness," Alex said.

"Ha, ha. I guess you think—" Stevie began, letting her guard down for an instant. Then she stopped herself. She refused to let Alex get a rise out of her. Freezing him out was her only hope of maintaining a last shred of dignity. Silently, though, she groaned. Two weeks! *Two weeks!* What was it about two weeks? Two weeks to get into shape. Two weeks to prepare a demonstration for Max. Two weeks till vacation ended. Didn't she have some homework or something? Better not think about it. . . . Who knew what awful assignments lurked in her backpack? Luckily it was safely zipped and stowed in the back of the closet.

"Look," Stevie said, finally giving in to an overwhelming urge to snap at her brother, "would you mind taking the fitness parade out to the kitchen so I can watch *Priced to Sell*? You're blocking my view."

"I've got a better idea," Alex said. He got down on the floor and began to do push-ups. "One! Two! Three! Hey, aren't you going to Pine Hollow? For some 'exercise'?" He snickered. "Won't Carole and Lisa be wondering where you are?"

Ignoring him, Stevie took the remote and turned the TV up. Normally she had no trouble with snappy comebacks. But this time Alex was right. Carole had probably been there for hours. Lisa would have joined her after breakfast. "What do you care?" she growled. Mentally, however, she was forced to cede round two to Alexander Lake.

6

CAROLE WAS FAR from Pine Hollow. She wasn't even in Willow Creek. She was two towns over, speeding along the back roads in Pat Naughton's sports car. And this, Carole thought happily, was the life.

"So anyway, Dave asked me what I most wanted for our tenth anniversary and I said, 'A horse.' I thought he was going to fall off his chair. But he's gotten used to the idea. He might even try riding himself. If I ever find a horse, that is."

"That's great. You guys could ride together," Carole said. She had always thought that being grown up looked pretty boring. But Pat made it seem fun. Carole was almost sorry when they pulled over to the side of the road

56

and parked in front of the house where their first appointment was.

The two of them had gotten out of the car and started toward the front door when a window was pushed open. A woman with her hair in curlers poked her head out. "Here about the horse?" she called.

"Why, yes," Pat said, walking toward the window. "I have a ten A.M. appointment to see . . ."—she consulted her day book briefly.

"I know, I know, you're here to see Princess. Well, you're too late. She was sold yesterday," the woman announced flatly.

"Sold?" Pat repeated.

"Yeah! Sold! You got a problem with that? Sold to a nice little girl over in Baker's Village."

Carole was ready to turn around and go, but Pat put her hands on her hips and stood her ground. "Excuse me, but I *called* yesterday and you said the horse was still available."

The woman shrugged and gave them a "What can you do?" look. "Hey, I didn't know if she'd pass the vet check. I mean, if anything fell through, you had a shot at her."

"Oh, *thanks*," said Pat, her voice dripping with sarcasm. "You mean you were willing to sell us a lame horse?"

"I didn't say she was lame!" the woman yelled, her face turning a nasty shade of red.

"What else would she be if she didn't pass the vet check?" Pat retorted.

"She did pass the vet check!" the woman shot back.

"Right: Sound on Saturday, lame on Sunday, I'll bet!"

"Look, you better get outa here or I'm gonna call the cops!" the woman said, brandishing a fist at them.

"Uh, Pat?" Carole said quietly. "Maybe we should save our energy for the next appointment."

Pat looked distractedly at Carole. Then all at once she burst out laughing. "You know what? You're right. I was having too much fun yelling."

As they headed back to the car, another car pulled up behind them. A man in breeches and boots got out. "Here to see the horse?" Pat asked.

"Uh, yeah," the man said uncertainly. He held up a tattered copy of *Horseman's Weekly*. "The one advertised."

"Too late," Pat said. "Sold yesterday."

"Sold yesterday!" the man exclaimed angrily. "Of all the rude—"

"Don't worry," Carole said, getting into the spirit of things. "Turns out it was lame anyway."

Shaking his head in disgust, the man thanked them, got into his car, and drove away.

Back in Pat's car, Carole was overcome with giggles. "I

never would have had the guts to chew that woman out. You were great!"

"It comes from years of practice," Pat said.

"My friend Stevie's good at that," Carole said. In a way, Pat reminded her of a grown-up Stevie, even though Stevie was a tomboy and Pat seemed so glamorous.

"Stevie Lake?" said Pat. "I know her. We live right down the road from the Lakes. I see you guys together a lot at Pine Hollow—with one other girl."

"Yeah, that's Lisa. We're The Saddle Club," Carole said.

"The Saddle Club?" Pat repeated.

Carole explained about the club. Pretty soon she found herself telling Pat about some of their adventures.

"Gosh, sounds like you guys are *tight*!" said Pat.

"We sure are," Carole agreed. But then her face fell. No doubt Stevie and Lisa were at Pine Hollow right then, joking and laughing, taking Belle and Prancer out, getting a jump start on their demonstrations for Max. With a twinge Carole thought of Starlight, waiting in his stall, expecting her to come. If she had said something to Stevie and Lisa, they would have taken him out. But Carole hadn't said anything. In fact, she had deliberately "forgotten" to call them last night. She had spent the evening worrying over the *Horseman's Weekly* story contest. Once Lisa had mentioned it, Carole did want to enter. The topic was a turning point in the life of a horse and rider. The thing was, it was hard to write about a turning point when she herself was riding the same horse she'd been riding for months and months and months. A horse she knew as well as any of her friends, as well as her father—maybe better. *If only I were looking for a horse,* Carole thought idly. *Then I'd have the perfect topic.*

"All right, here we are: the 'seasoned hunter,'" said Pat, turning onto a well-maintained driveway. "Let's keep our fingers crossed."

"Only one hand!" Carole reminded her. "Two is bad luck."

"Oops!" said Pat, uncrossing the fingers of one hand as they strode toward a small barn.

The barn had two stalls that opened onto a large paddock. It wasn't posh, but it was neat and practical. Carole and Pat looked at one another hopefully.

"Hello! Over here!" A girl in jeans who had a brown ponytail waved from the barn, beckoning them closer. She was grooming a large chestnut pony that stood on a pair of cross-ties. "Hello! You're here to see my pony, right?"

"Pony?" Pat asked uncertainly. "You mean the seasoned hunter?"

"Yeah—here he is. He's hunted three seasons and won loads of children's hunter trophies!" the girl said enthusiastically. "By the way, I'm Missy."

Pat and Carole shook hands with Missy. "So you're the one looking, right?" Missy said to Carole. Before Carole could answer, the girl had fetched a saddle and settled it on the back of the chestnut.

Carole looked at Pat. "What do we do?" she mouthed.

"Umm . . . I think there's some mistake," Pat said gently.

"A mistake?" the girl asked. "But you haven't even *tried* him yet. At least give Buster a chance!"

"No—No, he looks lovely," Pat assured her. "It's just that *I'm* the one looking."

"You?" Missy said, taking in Pat's five feet, nine inches. "But you're way too— Oh, no!" she cried as her face registered understanding. "Don't tell me they did it again!"

"Did what?" Carole inquired.

"It's the ad people at *Horseman's Weekly!*" Missy wailed. "They did this two weeks ago, too. They left out the *pony!*"

"Huh?" Carole and Pat said in unison.

" 'Seasoned *pony* hunter!' That's what the ad is supposed to say. Gosh darn it!"

Carole and Pat murmured sympathetically as Missy explained. "You see, the first time they messed up the height. They put fifteen point one instead of fourteen point one. I couldn't understand why no one was calling. Then I saw the ad. Nobody wants to buy a pony hunter that's the size of a horse!"

"You're right about that," Carole said. Officially, a pony was any horse that stood at or under fourteen hands, two inches. The measuring at horse shows was very strict. Obviously, you couldn't enter a fifteen-point-one-hand horse in pony classes: It would be considered illegal.

"So then what happened?" Pat asked.

"So then I took the height out entirely. But then *they* took out the *pony*—left it out, I mean. So I had four adults come look at him! Last week I finally got some kids. But now this!"

Pat nodded. "I'm sure we would have noticed if it had said 'pony hunter.'"

Missy looked glum. "I was hoping to sell him before school starts. Or not hoping. I don't want to sell him at all. But I'm getting a new horse in two weeks and he's got to be gone. We lease out the second stall to a boarder," she explained.

Carole and Pat chatted easily with Missy for a few minutes. Like most horsey people, they didn't need much to get them going. The topic of horses was endless. When they left, Missy was putting a bridle on Buster. "He's almost tacked up, so of course I'll ride now!" she said.

Carole smiled. That was exactly what she would have done.

As Pat had feared, the quiet beginner horse could barely get out of a walk. Their one-thirty appointment, on the other hand, had a bucking problem—as well as a rearing problem and a bolting problem. "Exaggerating is one thing!" Pat cried in exasperation. "But calling that horse 'trained' is—is—" She took a perturbed bite of her hamburger. "Words fail me, Carole, but it's wrong. It's just plain wrong!"

Carole nodded, her mouth full of fries. She and Pat were wolfing fast food on their way to the last appointment of the day. "If it's any consolation, it happens in reverse, too," she said. Briefly she recounted The Saddle Club's efforts to help find a suitable owner for Garnet, Veronica diAngelo's former horse. "She was a pretty little Arabian. And we had a three-hundred-pound woman show up who wanted to use her as a parade mount!"

Pat laughed appreciatively. "That's true—I've never been on that side of the fence. I've never had to sell a horse. When my horse got old we just put him out to pasture. How about you?" she asked Carole. "Have you ever gone through that?"

"No," Carole replied quietly. "Starlight is the only horse I've ever owned."

"And why you'd ever need another is beyond me," Pat remarked.

"I guess someday I'll have to move on," Carole said hesitantly. The thought was new to her. She'd never really considered her riding life after Starlight.

"He looks like he'd be so much fun to ride," said Pat.

Carole noticed the wistful tone in Pat's voice. "Why don't you try him sometime?" she offered generously.

"Are you sure?" Pat said. "I'd love to!"

"Tomorrow then. I insist," Carole added.

"I'll be there," Pat said. "It will be great after riding these horses. I just pray this last horse is good. He sure *sounds* promising."

"Which one is that?" Carole asked.

"King's Ransom," said Pat, "the warmblood dressage horse."

"Oh, right," Carole said, pretending to remember. In fact, she'd known all the time, all day, what their last appointment was. She could have recited the ad by heart, from "16.2 hand" to "ready to go all the way with the right rider." Getting out of the car, Carole fervently hoped the gelding wouldn't live up to his description. Then she could forget about him. Right now, for some reason, she couldn't.

"My gosh, he's even more unbelievable in real life!" Pat whispered. Both Carole and Pat had gasped aloud when they saw King. The owner, a young woman named Jenny, stood at the top of a wooded pasture and whistled. At this cue a large, dark brown horse lifted his head and came toward them, trotting, then cantering, his tail streaming out behind him.

"I always like people to see him in his natural habitat," Jenny remarked, slipping a leather halter over his elegant head. "That's how I first saw him—grazing in the fields in Holland."

"He's beautiful," Pat remarked.

Carole couldn't say a thing. King looked like her

dream horse—or a horse out of a fairy tale. But he was *real*.

After tacking him up, Jenny mounted to put him through his paces. Carole knew this was good etiquette: An owner should always ride the horse she was selling first. That way, if the horse was feeling frisky it would be obvious, and the potential buyer could be prepared for it. Of course it was also a great opportunity to show what the horse could do. And King could do plenty.

Jenny spent twenty minutes showing him off. The pair did extended trots and tiny canter circles. They leg-yielded. They did turns on the forehand. They went from a walk to a canter without trotting. They halted from a trot. The whole time, King's ears moved forward and back, listening. He looked like the dressage horses in photographs, perfectly collected, perfectly balanced.

"Anything else you want to see?" Jenny called.

"No, I'm ready to try him myself!" Pat said eagerly.

After giving Pat a leg up and helping her get settled, Jenny came over to the rail of the ring. Carole had been hoping she would. She relished any chance to talk with an advanced rider, and Jenny clearly fell into that category.

"King is gorgeous!" she blurted out. "Did you train him yourself?"

Jenny smiled at the compliment. "Not totally. He got a

66

good start overseas. But I took him up to the advanced levels."

Carole could hear the pride in Jenny's voice. "Where do you show him?" she asked.

Jenny named several of the largest dressage shows on the East Coast. "I really want him to find an owner who'll appreciate his talent," she said. She looked curiously at Carole. "Do you ride?"

"Yes, I have my own horse," Carole said.

"Do you do dressage?" Jenny inquired.

"I do, but not like you," Carole said. "You're a professional, aren't you?"

Jenny nodded. "Yeah. After I got out of college there wasn't anything else I wanted to do. So now I ride, show, teach, train horses—everything, really. I'm selling King because I can make a big profit on him. Besides, it's time to move on. I've taken him as far as I can." Apologetically, she added, "I know it sounds awfully cold, but when riding becomes a business, you have to be practical."

"Of course you do!" Carole agreed. She tried to assume a stern expression. *She* was going to be a professional, too, someday; she didn't want Jenny to think of her as some little Pony Clubber.

"Oops! He's acting up," Jenny commented.

Carole looked out to the ring. King had gotten his head down and was trying to buck. All Pat had to do was sit down firmly in the saddle and get the horse's head up. Instead she was letting the reins slide through her hands: a recipe for trouble.

"Get his head up!" Carole and Jenny cried at the same time.

They looked at each other and laughed. "Guess we think alike," Jenny called, hurrying out to assist Pat.

When King was settled, Pat asked if Jenny would mind setting up a few jumps. "I don't have any real jumps," Jenny said, sounding somewhat offended. "I'm a dressage rider, remember? But I tell you what, I'll line up these cavalletti."

Carole helped Jenny with the wooden Xs for the cavalletti. Then she asked to run in and use the bathroom. "Sure. It's just past the kitchen," said Jenny, pointing toward the house. "Make sure you check out the pictures of King!"

Carole was happy to oblige. She lingered in the hallway, taking in photo after photo of King under saddle, winning ribbons, and running free in the pasture.

When she returned, Pat had dismounted. "Not that I don't *like* dressage, don't get me wrong," she was saying to Jenny. She gave the horse a big pat. "Also, he's a little strong for me. Beautiful mover, though. . . . Hey, you ought to try him on the flat, Carole—just to see what he's like."

Carole caught her breath. "Could I?" she asked Jenny.

"Go ahead," said Jenny. "He needs the exercise."

Carole borrowed a hard hat from Pat and got on. As she rode off she heard Pat say, "Wait till you see what this girl can do."

King was even more amazing to ride than to watch. He was full of energy, but it was nothing Carole couldn't handle. Riding him was like soaring on air. At the slightest nudge from her heels or tightening of her hands on the reins, King would switch gaits. And every gait was better than the last. His trot *was* big and floating. His canter was rhythmic and powerful. As he trotted circles and figure eights and practiced flying lead changes, Carole lost all track of time. When she finally pulled him up, she was grinning so hard her face felt as if it would crack. She dismounted in a haze.

"You did beautifully with him!" Pat cried, rushing over. "Much better than I ever could."

"It was all King," Carole murmured.

"No—not everyone can handle him," said Jenny, adding, "You ride well."

King nuzzled Carole inquisitively as she handed over the reins. "Good boy," Carole said, patting him. "I hope you find a great owner. Thank you," she said quietly to Jenny. "That's a ride I'll never forget."

"Nor I," said Pat. "Even though I can't make you an offer."

"That's okay," said Jenny. "After all, I want him to go to somebody who will take him up to his full potential."

Pat began to say something but stopped. Carole wished they were alone. Then she could have explained that Jenny's comment was nothing personal. Any rider would stand up for her horse like that.

Together the three of them walked toward the stable. They helped Jenny untack King. Then, while Pat made a quick call home on her cellular phone, Carole hung over King's stall door. Jenny joined her.

"His conformation is nearly perfect," Carole marveled.

Jenny nodded absently. Then she gave Carole a curious look. "You really like him, don't you?" she said.

"Oh, yes," Carole breathed.

"*You're* not looking, are you?" Jenny asked suddenly.

Carole was taken aback. "Looking for a horse?" she said. "Me? Oh gosh, no! No, not at all. But thanks!"

"It's too bad," Jenny said with a shrug. "You'd make a great pair. You're just the kind of talented young rider I want for King. So *his* talent doesn't go to waste."

Dimly Carole was aware of Pat wrapping up her conversation. The same strange impulse as before seemed to take hold of her. "I mean, I don't *think* I'm looking," she heard herself say. "That is, unless I found some-thing . . ." She let her voice trail off vaguely.

Jenny scribbled on a piece of paper and pressed it into Carole's hand. "Here's my number," she said. "Come back any time."

TV WAS CATCHING. Or watching it was. Or something like that. It was funny, Stevie thought, how *Priced to Sell* faded into reruns of *Starship Attack* and *Starship Attack* faded into music videos and music videos faded into *Doctors' Hospital*. "I don't even *like Doctors' Hospital*," Stevie muttered, fiddling with the remote control. "I don't even like soap operas." Pessimistically she flipped through all the channels. Then she came back to *Doctors' Hospital*. "Alex! Will you bring me some chips and dip?" she yelled.

Alex appeared in a moment, bearing snacks. He and Stevie had gotten into a screaming, biting, clawing fight during *Starship Attack*. Now the air was clear. This was a pattern in the Lake household: After a big fight, the two feuding siblings would get along fine. Fortunately, the Lake parents were at work. Otherwise Stevie and Alex would have been sent to their rooms.

"Sour cream and onion, or barbecue?" Alex inquired.

"Barbecue, thank you," said Stevie. "Shhh . . . Dr. Bob is about to propose to Maria."

Two hours later, Stevie still had not moved. The phone rang and she grabbed the receiver. "Who would have the nerve to call during *Truth or Rumor?*" she said indignantly. "Hello?"

It was Lisa. "Have a good day?" she asked.

"Except for one thing," Stevie said. She recounted the morning race. "And so there's a rematch the Saturday after next," she finished, somewhat glumly.

Lisa, however, was all enthusiasm. "Stevie, that's great! You can start a fitness program tomorrow and beat him!"

"Hmmm," said Stevie, getting an inkling of what was coming.

"In fact," Lisa said, "I'll do it with you! I can be your coach—your personal trainer—your workout partner!"

"Great," said Stevie, dreading the thought. She knew all too well how Lisa loved a project, especially anything to do with self-improvement.

"It'll be fun! I can't wait to start, can you? Why don't I come over tomorrow morning?"

"I don't know about that, Lisa . . ." Stevie thought fast and came up with the perfect excuse. "Shouldn't we ride tomorrow morning?" she proposed.

"We can ride afterward—after the training session. In the afternoon if we have to."

"Is that when you rode today?" Stevie asked suddenly. "In the afternoon?"

72

"Why?" Lisa said warily. "Did you ride in the morning?"

"No. Remember? I was worn out from racing Alex."

"Well, I, uh, had a lot to do—homework, thank-you notes . . ."

"So you went in the afternoon?" Stevie repeated.

There was a pause at the other end. "All right, if you have to know, I didn't ride today, okay? Maybe it seems—"

"I didn't ride, either!" Stevie interrupted.

"You didn't?" said Lisa.

"Uh-uh. I, uh, had a lot of shows to watch."

Lisa laughed. "I went to TD's with my mom," she confessed.

"TD's!" Stevie exclaimed. "Without us?" The ice cream parlor was a favorite Saddle Club hangout.

Lisa laughed. "Sorry. Hey, let's conference-call Carole and see if she went to Pine Hollow."

"Are you kidding? Of course she went," Stevie said.

"You're probably right," agreed Lisa.

Stevie put Lisa on hold and dialed the Hansons' house. Sure enough, Colonel Hanson answered and said Carole wasn't home yet.

"Thanks," said Stevie. "I'll try her later."

"Naturally," said Lisa when Stevie told her. "She's probably helping Red muck out."

There was a silence. Each girl knew what the other was thinking. They ought to have gone to Pine Hollow, not only to ride but to help Red and Mrs. Reg with the stable chores. Stevie spoke first. "Uh, I better hang up. My mom will be home soon, and I'll be in big trouble if she thinks I watched TV all day."

"I have to go, too," Lisa said. "I've got to finish my English reading, needlepoint— But, hey," she added, remembering her new role as Stevie's coach, "I'll see you tomorrow, bright and early!"

After putting the phone down, Lisa stared up at her picture of The Saddle Club. Horse-crazy? she thought. They sure weren't acting like it. Willing to help each other out in any situation? While Carole was helping out Red and Mrs. Reg, the two of them were sitting at home. "But we always help out!" Lisa wailed. "Why can't someone else help out for a while?" The picture didn't answer. It just stared back at her accusingly. How long would she and Stevie go, it seemed to ask, breaking both rules of The Saddle Club?

IN HER DREAM Stevie was running. She was running along a road. She was wearing sweatpants and a sweatshirt. She had no memory of putting them on. And Lisa was there, too, running beside her. Lisa was saying something. What was it? Over her own panting breaths, Stevie could just make out her words. "Pick up your knees! Look sharp! Come on, here we go! One, two, one, two!" Stevie looked at her surroundings: bare trees, gray sky, houses, mailboxes. "It's not a dream!" she yelled.

"Of course it's not!" Lisa replied. "I just got you up and out running before you had time to realize you were awake."

"Gosh." Stevie was dumbfounded. She tried to sound

nonchalant when she asked, "What, ah—What time is it?"

"Six-forty-five! Hey, no lagging on this hill!" Lisa barked. "Move it! Move it!"

At the word *hill* Stevie felt her feet start to drag. Or maybe it was the realization that she was awake at the same time she normally got up for school. Either way, she slowed her pace. She was suddenly aware of a cramp in her side, a burning sensation in her lungs.

Lisa looked over at her trainee. She had to think of a way to keep her going. "Stevie?"

"Can't talk," Stevie panted. "No breath."

"Just nod then. You see that big oak tree way up in the distance?"

Stevie nodded.

"Imagine that tree is Alex. And he just insulted you. He told you riding wasn't a real sport. He told you— Hey!" Lisa yelled as Stevie lunged forward in a great burst of speed. "Wait for me!"

Back at the house, Lisa critiqued Stevie's performance. They had jogged two miles. Stevie had moaned and groaned for one and a half. "But you did it without stopping," Lisa conceded, "and I'm proud of you."

Stevie couldn't answer. She was too busy draining a huge plastic jug of water. "Pheweeeee! That wasn't so bad. Now let's eat."

Lisa looked doubtful. "You want to eat before your push-ups and sit-ups?" she asked.

"Push-ups?" said Stevie, refilling her jug. "And sit-ups?"

Before Lisa could answer, Alex, Michael, and Chad traipsed into the kitchen. Alex was all in spandex. Michael and Chad were in pajamas, rubbing their eyes. "Do you always have to wake us up?" Michael grumbled at Alex.

"Yeah, with all that *whistling*?" Chad said disgustedly.

"It's just I have so much energy that I wake up in a good mood and I— *Hel*-lo!" Alex said, taking in Stevie and Lisa. The three boys stared at them.

"I didn't know you slept over, Lisa," said Chad.

"I didn't," Lisa said, giggling at Chad's sheepish look. She and Chad had once gone on a couple of dates. Nothing had come of it, but it still made for the occasional awkward moment. Especially, Lisa thought, when she caught Chad in his pajamas!

"You see, *we* don't have a problem getting up early," Stevie said pointedly. "We're used to it—from going to horse shows."

"Ha, ha," said Alex. "What did you do, Lisa, pour a pitcher of water over her head?"

"Actually I—"

"Pitcher of water? Don't you mean jug?" Stevie cried.

In a flash she dumped hers over Alex's head. "Come on, Lisa!"

The two girls thundered up the stairs. They ran into Stevie's room and slammed the door. A moment later there was a knock. "You can't come in!" Stevie yelled.

"Oh, can't I?" said a stern voice.

Grinning wanly, Stevie opened the door. "Ah—Hi, Mom."

Mrs. Lake stood there dressed for work. Somehow she managed to frown at Stevie and give Lisa a welcoming smile at the same time.

"I thought I heard your voice, Lisa. And what, may I ask, are you two doing up to so early?" said Mrs. Lake.

"Working out, of course," Stevie answered. At her mother's surprised look she added, "It so happens that Alex and I have a little contest in two weeks."

"Aha! So that's why you're preoccupied with athletic activity," Mrs. Lake said knowingly. "Good old sibling rivalry."

"Oh, no, Mom," Stevie said sternly. "I'm getting into shape because, uh, everyone ought to exercise regularly. Good for the heart—you know—lungs, respiratory tract, calf muscles. Et cetera."

Mrs. Lake smiled. "Try my abs and arms video," she offered.

A vivid image came to Stevie's mind of her mother panting on the family room floor, cursing at a leotard-clad woman on TV. "I don't know, Mom. It's nice of you to offer, but—"

"That sounds great, Mrs. Lake!" Lisa broke in. "Is it hard?"

"It's a killer," Mrs. Lake promised. She wished the girls a good day and turned to go. "Oh, and Stevie," she added, "after that video?"

"Yeah, Mom?"

"The TV goes off!"

Stevie had never known exactly where her abdominals were. After the video, she still didn't know: Her entire torso was in agony. So was her neck. Even one of her ankles felt odd. And her arms felt like dead weights. "I think I'm gonna puke," she said hoarsely.

"Nonsense!" said Lisa, all business. "Here. I have a pad of paper."

"What else is new?" Stevie muttered.

Lisa was known for her organizational skills. She whipped out a ballpoint pen. "Tell me what your fitness goals are and I'll make a list."

"I have only one goal," Stevie whispered. "To live till tomorrow."

In spite of herself Lisa laughed. While Stevie lay belly-aching on the couch, Lisa mapped out a schedule of everything they had to do over the next ten days to beat Alex. On one level Lisa was worried: Stevie's inherent laziness wasn't going to help matters. But in the end they'd be just fine. Stevie's insane competitive streak would win out.

"All right, jock, time for breakfast."

Instantly Stevie revived. "Let's make bacon!" she yelled.

The girls fried some bacon and tried to make omelettes, which quickly turned into scrambled eggs. They were talking and laughing. But the moment they sat down to eat, both of them got very quiet. Lisa noticed that they were avoiding each other's eyes. She had the feeling they were both thinking the same thing—the same thing as each other, and the same thing as last night on the phone.

"I guess we really ought to map out a schedule for Belle and Prancer, too, huh, Stevie?"

Stevie nodded. Lisa was right. Here it was, their third day of not riding. Carole probably thought they were lazy beyond belief. But still, Stevie reminded herself, the day was young. "Look, we can go to Pine Hollow right after *Priced to Sell*."

Lisa perked up at once. "Excellent idea. We'll take a little break and then head out. After that workout, we deserve a break!" They cleaned up and headed into the family room.

Chad, however, had already claimed the TV. He was watching music videos.

"But *Priced to Sell* is on!" Stevie wailed.

"Tough. I hate game shows," Chad said. "And I'll be gone in an hour. Dan's coming over and we're going to the mall to get computer stuff."

"Dan's driving you to the mall?" Stevie said plaintively.

"Yup."

Stevie and Lisa looked at one another. An excursion to the mall would be fun!

"Can we come?"

Chad took his eyes off the screen to survey them briefly. "Okay. As long as you don't say *one* word about working out! Alex is already driving me crazy with his power shakes and his body mass index. I just don't care, got it?"

"Got it," Stevie said solemnly. She turned to Lisa, all thoughts of riding forgotten. "Come on, let's go call Carole and see if she can come!"

CAROLE FOLLOWED THE horse and rider with her eyes. They were going at a trot. The horse was moving well; the rider rose naturally in the saddle. "Nice job, Pat!" she called. "Why don't you try a canter?"

"Great!"

Carole saw Pat sit down to ask for the transition. She

leaned forward slightly and Starlight broke into a canter. Pat's face lit up. "Gosh, he's well-behaved!"

"Knock on wood!" Carole joked.

Twenty minutes later Pat rode into the center of the ring, her face still ecstatic. "You've trained him so well!" she exclaimed. "He's perfect!"

Carole smiled. "I don't know about perfect," she said, "but thanks."

"Say, would you mind if I tried a jump?" Pat asked.

"Not at all," Carole replied readily. It would be good for Starlight to hop over a few fences. "I'll drag that cross rail and vertical into place."

While she set up two low jumps, Carole saw Pat rubbing Starlight's neck and praising him. Starlight pranced along happily. It was strange, but for a moment, watching them, Carole felt left out. A twinge of sadness passed through her. Pat's enthusiasm reminded her of how she used to feel about Starlight. Lately she couldn't seem to make him do anything right. What had changed?

Jumping Starlight only made Pat more enthusiastic. She trotted the cross rail and cantered over the vertical a number of times. "I just can't get over how great this horse is," she gushed, pulling up and dismounting. "Are you going to ride now? I'd love to see what he can really do."

Carole hesitated. She was tired; she'd had a fitful

night's sleep and didn't feel much like riding. But what could she do, say no? To riding her own horse? *That* would look strange. And Carole wanted to explain her mood even less than she wanted to ride. Reluctantly she traded places with Pat.

From the moment she gathered up the reins, Carole realized her mistake. She should have trusted her instincts. Starlight could sense what kind of mood she was in. It was almost as if he *wanted* to make her look bad in front of Pat. He wouldn't walk, he wouldn't halt, he hedged away from one corner of the indoor ring—every time they passed it. "Would you behave?" Carole muttered through clenched teeth. As she drew near the door, she saw Mrs. Reg standing with Pat, watching her intently.

Having Max's mother there annoyed Carole. It made her nervous, though normally she wouldn't have cared. *I'll show them*, she thought. She turned Starlight toward the vertical. As they approached, the wind whistled through the rafters of the roof. Starlight shied violently and ducked out of line. He got the bit between his teeth and bolted.

Carole was so stunned she couldn't react right away. Her champion jumper had *run out* before a fence! That was one of the worst faults there was. At last she sat back in the saddle and reined him in. She brought him back to a trot and made a circle. Her face burning with shame, Carole reapproached the jump. Starlight ran out again.

The third time, Carole was ready. She opened her outside rein and used her inside leg. She made Starlight go forward. He dodged right and left. Finally he got in under the fence and popped it. The awkward jump unseated Carole. She managed to hang on, but barely. When she had recovered herself, she was embarrassed beyond belief. She didn't want to ride anymore. She also didn't want to ride over to Pat and Mrs. Reg.

"I'd better call it a day!" she yelled.

"All right!" Pat called anxiously. "I hope I didn't mess him up!"

"No—oh, no; you didn't do anything wrong!" Carole assured her, her voice choked with shame.

As she slowed to a walk, she heard Mrs. Reg asking Pat if she would like to ride Barq and Pat saying she would. The two women left the side of the ring together.

Only then did Carole dare dismount. She halted right away and got off. How could she have made such a fool of herself? In front of Pat, her new friend, and Mrs. Reg, who would probably tell Max! Fighting off tears of frustration, Carole dejectedly led Starlight to his stall. She untacked him as quickly as possible and went to the tack room.

Mrs. Reg was inside, straightening up. Carole looked at

the floor, humiliated. "Say, where are your other two thirds?" Mrs. Reg asked.

"Huh? Oh—Stevie and Lisa? They must be coming this afternoon," Carole said. She was so upset, she hadn't even noticed their absence. Anyway, she was glad they hadn't been around to witness her second horrible performance. First the lesson and now this.

"Bad day?" Mrs. Reg asked quietly. When Carole didn't answer, she said gently, "Everyone has them sometimes."

Carole's frown only deepened. She wasn't in the mood for the older woman's cheery wisdom.

"The other day," Mrs. Reg went on, oblivious, "I was in a bad mood because I had to clean out my attic. But you know what? It paid off. I found a dress up there that I hadn't seen in a long time. It was a dress I'd made myself. I wore it, oh, for years. Everyone complimented me on this dress, and I was very proud of it. It was blue gingham with— Well, never mind. The fabric's not important. The point is, I found it again! I was so excited because I thought I had passed it on ages ago. Now I can't wait to start wearing it again. Funny how that works, isn't it? You think you're through with something and then—"

"Mrs. Reg?" Carole broke in. "Can I use the phone?"

Mrs. Reg paused in midsentence. She gave Carole a searching look. The phone in Max's office was to be used

85

only for very important calls. "If you need to, dear . . . Yes, of course you can," she said.

Carole fled the room before Mrs. Reg could change her mind. She ran to the office and drew a slip of paper from her pocket. Her hands were trembling. She dialed the number. After several rings, Jenny picked up. "Sorry!" the older girl said breathlessly. "I was in the barn!"

"It's Carole Hanson," Carole said, getting right to the point. "I—I was wondering if I could come ride King again."